This book should be returned to any branch of the
Lancashire County Library on or before the date shown

2 2 AUG 2017
1 4 SEP 2017

1 2 OCT 2017
- 8 DEC 2017

0 5 MAR 2018
2 9 MAR 2018
0 5 JUN 2018
1 5 AUG 2018

Other titles by Holly Webb

The Hounds of Penhallow Hall:
The Moonlight Statue

Winter Stories:

The Snow Bear

The Reindeer Girl

The Winter Wolf

The Storm Leopards

The Snow Cat

Animal Stories:

Lost in the Snow

Alfie all Alone

Lost in the Storm

Sam the Stolen Puppy

Max the Missing Puppy

Sky the Unwanted Kitten

Timmy in Trouble

Ginger the Stray Kitten

Harry the Homeless Puppy

Buttons the Runaway Puppy

Alone in the Night

Ellie the Homesick Puppy

Jess the Lonely Puppy

Misty the Abandoned Kitten

Oscar's Lonely Christmas

Lucy the Poorly Puppy

Smudge the Stolen Kitten

The Rescued Puppy

The Kitten Nobody Wanted

The Lost Puppy

The Frightened Kitten

The Secret Puppy

The Abandoned Puppy

The Missing Kitten

The Puppy Who was Left Behind

The Kidnapped Kitten

The Scruffy Puppy

The Brave Kitten

The Forgotten Puppy

The Secret Kitten

A Home for Molly

Sammy the Shy Kitten

The Seaside Puppy

The Curious Kitten

Monty the Sad Puppy

Maisie Hitchins:

The Case of the Stolen Sixpence

The Case of the Vanishing Emerald

The Case of the Phantom Cat

The Case of the Feathered Mask

The Case of the Secret Tunnel

The Case of the Spilled Ink

The Case of the Blind Beetle

The Case of the Weeping Mermaid

The Homeless Kitten

Holly Webb

Illustrated by Sophy Williams

For everyone who has adopted a cat or kitten from a shelter – you are fabulous!

www.hollywebbanimalstories.com

STRIPES PUBLISHING
An imprint of the Little Tiger Group
1 The Coda Centre, 189 Munster Road,
London SW6 6AW

A paperback original
First published in Great Britain in 2017

Text copyright © Holly Webb, 2017
Illustrations copyright © Sophy Williams, 2017
Author photograph copyright © Nigel Bird

ISBN: 978-1-84715-783-6

The right of Holly Webb and Sophy Williams to be
identified as the author and illustrator of this work
respectively has been asserted by them in accordance
with the Copyright, Designs and Patents Act, 1988.

Chapter One

"You're coming with me, Lily? Are you sure?" Dad grinned at her, widening his eyes and pretending to be shocked.

"I like the sound of a walk with you and Hugo in the woods. It'll be nice and cool under the trees. Anyway –" Lily made a face back at him – "I'd come with you more often if you didn't go so fast. You've both got really long legs and I haven't." Lily reached down to rub the dog's soft creamy white ears. "Yes, you do, don't you? Great big long legs." She looked up at Dad. "You're not planning on one of your five-mile hikes, are you?" she asked suspiciously.

Dad laughed. "No, not in this weather – it's too hot for a long walk now. Anyway, I took Hugo out running with me early this morning."

Lily nodded. Hugo needed loads of exercise. Dad took him for at least two long walks every day and he usually went for a quick walk in the park with Mum when she stopped working to take a lunch break. At weekends Dad often took Hugo in the car to the hills just outside town for a really good run. Lily's big sister, Carly, loved to go with them but Lily wasn't so keen. It always seemed to rain when she went on one of Dad's big days out.

Hugo was mostly German Shepherd – nobody was quite sure what else. Carly had told her that German Shepherds were originally bred from dogs trained to guard flocks of sheep from wolves and bears. They were used to working hard. Dad had wanted a really energetic dog and he'd fallen in love with Hugo at the animal shelter. He was so unusual with his white coat. The shelter staff said that Hugo had got too big for his elderly owner to look after properly – and at the time he hadn't even stopped growing.

Mum and Dad had explained to Lily and Carly that they'd have to be really gentle with him as he was a rescue dog, and because white German Shepherds could be quite sensitive and nervous. They were no good as pets for people who were out at work all day – if they were left alone they could end up wrecking a house because they were so miserable! Luckily, Mum worked at home as a graphic designer so Hugo was never by himself for long.

"Is Carly coming?" Dad asked. "Shout up the stairs for her, Lily."

"No, Mum's taking her round to Maisie's house in a minute. Maisie's got one of those giant paddling pools in her garden." Lily sighed enviously. It was the first week of the summer holidays and the weather was already so hot.

Even though it was sweltering, Hugo was still keen for his walk. He was standing by the front door staring at them both, his gleaming blue eyes hopeful. One of the boys in Carly's class had told her that Hugo was a spooky wolf dog because of his white coat and blue eyes, and Carly had got into trouble for chasing the boy round the playground. She adored Hugo even more than Dad did and Hugo loved her to bits.

Dad clipped on Hugo's lead and opened the front door. Hugo pulled Dad eagerly down the path, keen to be off, and Lily quickly slipped on her trainers and hurried after them. "Bye, Mum! See you later, Carly!"

As they turned out of the gate, Hugo suddenly stiffened, his ears pricking forward and his tail flicking from side to side.

Dad peered over the fence, where Hugo was looking. "What are you so excited about? Oh! No, Hugo, no chasing cats."

"Is it Pixie?" Lily ran down the path to look. "Hello, sweetheart!" Pixie was a gorgeous silvery tabby cat who belonged to their next-door neighbour, Anna. Lily loved to play with Pixie – so much that Carly was always teasing her about it. Everyone else in the family preferred dogs but Lily's room was full of cat posters and cat books... Even her pyjamas had kittens on them.

Luckily for Lily, Pixie was always popping into their garden. Sometimes she even walked along the garden wall, and then hopped on to the garage roof and in through Lily's bedroom window. Lily loved to pretend that Pixie was hers but Mum always shooed the cat out whenever she saw her. She said it wasn't fair on Hugo, letting a cat into his house.

Now the tabby cat was perched on the fence, looking down disapprovingly at Hugo, her tail swishing. Hugo had never chased Pixie but Lily thought he secretly wanted to. He didn't like her walking across his garden. He always stared at her out of the long windows in the living room, his nose pressed up against the glass. If Pixie hung around for too long, Hugo would let out a series of mighty barks.

Pixie rubbed her head against Lily's cheek, glared at Hugo and jumped back down to the other side of the fence. Hugo barked and wagged his tail excitedly.

"Come on, boy," Dad said gently. "Walk time. Off to the woods."

Hugo shook himself and loped out on to the pavement, Dad and Lily jogging after him. The little woods they were going to weren't far away – just a short walk up the hill.

"Ohhh, that's nice." Lily sighed happily, lifting her hair up off the back of her neck as they walked under the trees. "It's so much cooler here in the shade. Look, Hugo likes it, too. He must be so hot with all that thick fur."

Dad nodded. "I think this is one of Hugo's favourite places. So many good smells and all those squirrels."

"And sticks." Lily grinned. Hugo loved it when they threw sticks for him to chase after. "Are you going to let him off the lead?"

Dad looked around thoughtfully. Hugo was really good about coming back when he was called but because he was so big they had to be careful about letting him loose in case people were scared of him.

"I can't see anyone else… Yes, we'll let him off for the minute. It's more fun for him sniffing around in the bracken off the lead."

As Hugo ambled ahead, Lily and Dad chatted about what they were going to do over the summer. They'd gone on a brilliant holiday to a water park in half-term, so they weren't going away.

"I want to sort out the garden shed," Dad told Lily. "It's so full of junk, I can hardly get the lawnmower out."

"That's not very exciting!" Lily said, laughing. "You'll have to be careful though, Dad, have you seen the size of the spiders in that shed? I went in there yesterday to get the water guns and I'm sure I saw one the size of my hand."

"Mmm. I might wear gloves." Dad wrinkled his nose. "I suppose we should head back, it's almost time for lunch. Hugo! Come on, boy!"

Hugo was a little way away, gazing

curiously through the bracken, his tail wagging.

"Has he seen another dog?" Dad wondered, hurrying over. "Oh! Honestly. That's awful!"

"What is it?"

"Someone's dumped a load of stuff here, instead of taking it to the tip." Dad pointed to a pile of furniture – an old sofa and a fridge and what looked like some kitchen units. "What a mess! I'll have to ring the council when we get home, see if they'll come and take it away. I suppose the woods do back on to all those houses. Someone must have driven down the alleyway to the garages – yes, look, the fence is broken. It wouldn't have been too hard to get the stuff through here."

"That's really sad." Lily looked at the mess, frowning. "Hey, Hugo. Where are you going, silly? That's not a sofa for sitting on!" Hugo wasn't supposed to sit on any sofas but it was his one bad habit. He would lie at Dad's feet with his nose on the sofa, and gradually creep further and further forward until he could sneak his front paws on. He never got very far before he was pushed off – but he never gave up trying, either. He just wanted to be snuggled up with his family.

"Here, boy, come on," Dad called. "Hugo!"

But Hugo didn't come back like he usually did. He was sniffing at the old sofa, his plumy tail swishing really fast.

"Maybe it smells of food," Dad said, edging his way through the bracken to follow him. "It must smell of something, look at him, he's really excited. Hugo, leave it, come on!"

Hugo's ears were pricked right forward now, and he was whining and grunting and sniffing at the tatty sofa cushions.

Lily went after Dad, wriggling sideways through the undergrowth – she only had shorts on and there were nettles in among the bracken but she wanted to see what Hugo was so excited about.

Hugo had his nose down the back of the sofa cushions now. Then suddenly he jumped back with a snort.

"What is it?" Lily asked, leaning

over – and then she gasped.

Between the cushions and the back
of the sofa was a squirming mass of fur.
A litter of tiny, fluffy kittens!

Chapter Two

"Kittens!" Lily gasped. "Oh, wow! Did Hugo smell them? Or maybe he heard something?"

The kittens were squirming around, making tiny breathy squeaking noises. Hugo had moved the seat cushion with his nose while he was sniffing them out, so their cosy dark nest had been disturbed. Now the big dog was staring down at the kittens with his ears pricked right forward again. Dad had put a hand on his collar, just in case. After all, Hugo really didn't like Pixie, so it made sense that he wouldn't like the kittens, either. But right now he looked interested rather than grumpy.

Lily crouched down next to Hugo so she could look, too. There were three kittens – two tabbies and a gorgeous, little white kitten. Their fur looked quite long and fluffy to Lily, longer than Pixie's, she was sure. Perhaps they were going to be longhairs – like Persians. But they didn't have squashed Persian noses.

"I don't understand." Lily looked around. "Why would anyone put kittens down the back of a sofa? They should have taken them to an animal shelter, not just dumped them in the woods. It's a horrible thing to do!"

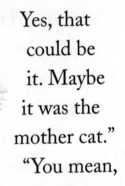

Dad nodded. "It is weird. Unless… Yes, that could be it. Maybe it was the mother cat."

"You mean, she had her babies out here in the woods?" Lily looked doubtful. Why would a cat want to have kittens in a grubby old sofa?"

"Cats do pick funny places sometimes. Grandma's cat had a litter of kittens in her wardrobe when she was a little girl, I remember her telling me."

22

"But why the woods instead of at home?" Lily looked up at Dad anxiously. "Maybe the mum doesn't have a home. Do you think she might be a stray?"

"Could be," Dad agreed. He glanced around, peering through the trees. "I wonder where she is. They look too small to be left alone for very long."

Just then the white kitten wriggled round and let out a squeaky little mew. Lily laughed delightedly. He – or she – was so cute, with a tiny pink nose and blue eyes. Even though his eyes were open, Lily didn't think he could really see her – his eyes didn't seem to be focusing. He was weaving his head about though, snuffing at the air. Lily wondered if he could smell Hugo.

Or perhaps he was just upset that their mum was gone and their nest had been disturbed.

"If their eyes are open, that means they've got to be a few days old, doesn't it?" Lily said, trying to think. She'd read somewhere that kittens were born with their eyes closed.

"Ye-ees." Dad nodded. "I guess so. But I'm still pretty sure they need their mum. They're too young to be walking around – they're just squirming about and wriggling on top of each other, aren't they?" He looked around again. "There's no sign of the mother cat. I wonder what it's best to do."

"Don't you think we should take them home, Dad?" Lily said pleadingly. "We can't leave them out here on their own, not when they're so little. They can't find any food for themselves, can they? Don't they still need their mum's milk?"

Dad shook his head. "Their mum could just have gone looking for food – she might be back any minute. Or maybe she actually *is* around here somewhere but she's too scared of us to come back to her kittens. I mean, no cat's going to walk up to Hugo…"

Hugo was still watching the kittens as though they were the best thing he'd seen in ages. He was following them with his nose as they clambered over and around each other, still squeaking.

"I think he likes them," Lily said, smiling. But then her smile faded. "What are we going to do, Dad? We can't just leave them and hope their mum comes back. What if she doesn't? They *need* her. Or somebody to look after them, anyway."

Dad frowned. "You know what? I'm going to ring the animal shelter where we got Hugo. I've got their number in my phone. I bet they'll know what to do."

Lily nodded. That was definitely a good idea. The staff at the shelter must have to deal with abandoned kittens all the time. She listened as her dad called up and explained about the kittens.

"No, we haven't seen the mum at all. Do you think she won't come back while we're here? No, I suppose not, if she's a stray… So, what do you think, should we leave them?"

"Oh no…" Lily whispered to herself, looking over at the tiny kittens. The little white one had ended up underneath the other two now. Lily longed to pick him up – surely it couldn't be good for him to be squashed like that?

She breathed a sigh of relief as he

wriggled out and accidentally nudged Hugo's nose with his own. Hugo stepped back, surprised, and Lily giggled.

"You like them, don't you?" Lily whispered to Hugo as he rested his chin on the arm of the sofa, gazing at the kittens.

Lily turned back to Dad. Surely the shelter couldn't be telling him to leave the kittens here? She couldn't bear to think of them all on their own.

"I'm really not sure how long she's been away, that's the thing," her dad was saying. "Amberdale Woods, that's right. Mmmm. Yes, we could do that. Will there be someone answering the phone later this evening? OK, I'll get back to you then. Thanks."

"What did they say?" Lily burst out.

"They think the mum's probably right here somewhere, hiding out and watching till we go away."

"Oh…" Lily looked around the woods, golden and silent in the sunlight. "But what if she's not? What if she doesn't come back?"

"Well, that's the problem. If she doesn't, I'm afraid the kittens won't last long without her. They're just too little to survive by themselves. They'll have to be taken to the shelter for hand-rearing – that means someone feeding them with a special bottle. So, we need to see what happens."

Dad made an apologetic face at Lily. "I said we'd keep an eye on them and watch out for their mum, Lils. It might be a bit boring. The lady from the shelter said we needed to give the mother cat a few hours before we do anything like moving the kittens."

"I don't mind! I don't want to leave them – even Hugo doesn't, look at him."

Dad nodded. "He's really fascinated,

isn't he? It's funny when you think how he is about Pixie. Maybe he doesn't understand that these are cats, too…" He smiled at Lily. "It's OK. I'm sure the mum will turn up soon if we get out of her way. Come on, Hugo," He looked around the clearing as Hugo paced slowly over to his side. "So now we need to find somewhere to watch from."

Lily stepped back reluctantly from the sofa and the kittens. The white kitten was on the top of the pile now, weaving his head from side to side. She longed to pick him up and cuddle him, and tell him everything was going to be OK but she knew she mustn't…

The white kitten mewed, calling miserably for his mother. He wanted milk – he kept blundering about, trying to suck but she wasn't there. He didn't understand. She had always been there to feed him before. She seemed to have been gone for so long and he was so hungry.

He hooked his tiny claws into the fabric at the back of the sofa and hauled himself up, sniffing the air, trying to find his mother. There was no warm, milky smell but he *could* smell something else, something different. He mewed uncertainly and sniffed the air again. The smell seemed to have moved away. Confused and worn out by the effort, he nuzzled into the furry pile of other kittens and settled back to sleep.

Chapter Three

"Lily, are you sure you don't want to go home?" Dad asked. "Mum just texted. She says she can walk up and get you and take Hugo back, too. We've been watching for an hour now. You must be getting hungry – it's past lunchtime."

Lily shook her head firmly. "I don't want to go home. And I don't mind not having any lunch."

They were sitting on a fallen tree with Hugo at their feet, just close enough to see the abandoned sofa through the bracken. Lily was pretty sure they were far enough away not to worry the mother cat, as long as they were quiet. The sofa wasn't that far from the main paths through the wood, so she must have been coming

and going with people and dogs
around.

"Please, Dad," Lily begged, as Dad
started to text Mum back. "I really
want to stay and make sure the kittens
are OK. I know we've been here an
hour but that's a whole hour that their
mum hasn't come back to look after
them. That can't be right, can it? She's
been gone ages."

Dad nodded. "It does seem a long time to me but I'm not really sure how often tiny kittens need to be fed. I don't think we can stay here all day, Lily. Perhaps we can keep popping back to check on them."

"But there's so many people who walk their dogs in this wood," Lily pointed out. "I know Hugo just wants to look at the kittens but another dog might hurt them."

They'd seen quite a few dog walkers already but luckily none of the dogs had come close enough to sniff out the kittens. Dad had asked the owners if they'd seen a cat around but they'd all said no. One lady had even offered to go home and ring the RSPCA when Dad and Lily told her about the kittens but Dad had explained they'd already called the shelter.

"OK," Dad said, putting his phone away. "I've told Mum we'll stay."

"What do you think could have happened to their mum?" Lily asked, a little while later. "I don't think she's coming back, Dad. Why would she leave them?"

Dad sighed. "I don't know. Perhaps she just couldn't look after them properly. The lady from the shelter did say that if a very young cat has kittens, they do sometimes abandon them. Because they just haven't got the energy to feed themselves and make enough milk for the kittens, too. If she's a stray and she's having to hunt for her food, or steal it out of bins, she might not be able to cope."

"That's so sad." Lily sighed, thinking of Pixie next door – so plump and well fed.

"Or it could be that she's not a stray. Maybe she just came here to have her kittens, and now her family have found her and they're keeping her in to stop her going off again."

"But they must know the kittens need her!" Lily shook her head. "Nobody would be that mean!"

Dad nodded. "No, you're probably right. I'm sure the owners would want to look after the kittens, too. Unless maybe they didn't realize she was pregnant...?"

Dad looked over towards the gap in the fence and the alleyway that led down to the houses and frowned. "Lily, listen, love. I don't want to upset you but there is another thing that could have happened. It's quite a busy road out there. She could have been hit by a car."

Lily swallowed and her voice wobbled when she answered. "I know. I was thinking that. We go down that road to school and cars do go really fast along there. Do you think she tried to cross it?"

"If she doesn't come back we'll probably never know." Dad put his arms round her shoulders. "But it's a possibility."

"Poor cat," Lily whispered. "And poor kittens."

"Well, at least we found them, thanks to Hugo."

"He's a hero." Lily rubbed his nose and Hugo turned to look back at her for a moment. Then his ears twitched and he stood up, gazing down the path. "Someone's coming," Lily murmured. "Oh, it's Mum! And Carly! But I said I didn't want to go back, Dad."

"Hello!" Lily's mum stood on tiptoe, trying to see the sofa and the kittens. "We thought we'd come and bring you some sandwiches. Are they over there?"

"Can I go and see?" Carly asked.

"Just quickly," Dad suggested. "We're watching for their mum, Carly. We don't want to scare her off."

As Mum and Carly hurried over to take a quick look, Hugo stood up, whining a little.

"It's OK, boy." Dad patted him reassuringly. "He really is keeping watch over those kittens, isn't he?"

"They're beautiful," Mum whispered, as she and Carly came creeping back through the bracken. "But so tiny! Surely they're going to need feeding soon?"

Dad nodded. "I reckon so. But the lady at the shelter told us not to do anything until this evening. Just watch and wait."

"Lily, you're sure you don't want to come home with us? You've been out here for hours."

Lily shook her head. "Not yet, Mum, please. I'm so worried about them – and their mum," she added sadly. "Dad thinks she might have been run over."

"Oh, Lily." Mum hugged her.

"It's so lucky that Hugo sniffed them out," Lily murmured.

"I was going to say that we'd take him back," Mum said thoughtfully. "But looking at him, I'm not sure he'd come. He's had his eyes fixed on that sofa the whole time since we arrived.

Maybe he thinks that because he found the kittens he's got to look after them." She was smiling but she sounded half-serious.

Lily nodded. "German Shepherds are often guard dogs, aren't they? Hugo's guarding the kittens."

Chapter Four

Lily leaned forward eagerly, certain she'd seen a flash of white close by the old sofa. Perhaps the kittens' mum was a white cat – that would make sense. She started to say, "Dad…" but then she sighed. It wasn't the cat, after all. Just an old plastic bag, flapping in the breeze.

She shivered a little. Even though

it had been such a hot day, the woods were shady, especially now the sun was starting to go down. She peered over at the sofa, wondering if the kittens were feeling chilly, too. She and Dad had gone to check on them after Mum and Carly had left, and pulled the cushion back over them a little but she couldn't help worrying.

Over in the clearing, the white kitten huddled closer to his sisters, hunting for some warmth. Usually they were all snuggled up together against their mother but without her body heat the kittens were so small that they couldn't keep themselves warm. He was getting colder and colder, and it was getting hard to move. He squeaked for his mother again, calling to her to come back and feed them but she didn't come. Exhausted and hungry, the tiny kitten tried to crawl further under the cushions.

Lily shifted position again. She was getting pins and needles from sitting still for so long, and she was hungry. The sandwiches Mum had brought seemed a long time ago. She checked her watch. "Dad, it's six o'clock," she murmured, stretching out her feet and wriggling a bit.

"I know. I'm going to phone the shelter. It's been seven hours now." He took out his phone and Lily leaned closer to try to listen in.

"Hi, I rang earlier about some kittens our dog had found in Amberdale Woods. No, no sign of their mum coming back, I'm afraid. Would you be able to come and get them?"

He paused for a minute or so, listening, and Lily saw an anxious expression appear on his face – little creases over the top of his nose. "Oh… No, don't do that. Maybe we can help? Look, give me a minute. Let me talk to my wife and get back to you." He listened for a little longer, saying, "Mm-hm, mm-hm," and Lily squeezed even closer, desperate to know what was going on.

"Dad, what's happened?" she burst out, as soon as he ended the call.

"The shelter's really full. All of their foster carers have got kittens already. The manager was saying she'd ring round and see who could squeeze them in. Apparently this is kitten season." He laughed a little nervously.

"So what's going to happen to our kittens?" Lily asked. "Will they go to one of these foster people? Will they be all right?"

Dad was silent for a minute, running his hand down the back of Hugo's neck. "Actually, Lily, I'm wondering if we could take them. Just until they can find someone to foster them properly."

"What?" Lily squeaked. She was so surprised and excited she actually jumped up and down. "Do you mean it? We can take them home?"

"Hold on! Slow down a minute. I'm only talking about us looking after them until there's space for them with a foster carer. Since it's an emergency. And I said I'd have to talk to your mum about it. There's no point getting excited just yet."

"I know." Lily's voice was shaking. Those tiny kittens, hers to look after! If only Mum would say yes! She watched eagerly as Dad called home.

"Sarah, it's me. Yes, I called them but there's a problem – apparently they're really full. The lady I spoke to earlier on didn't realize but all their kitten fosterers have got litters of kittens. No, we're not going to leave them, listen! What do you think about us looking after them for a bit? The shelter manager – she's the one I just spoke to – said she'd send someone out to help us take them home. They'll bring some kitten formula and some information sheets on how to care for them if we agree."

He went quiet for a bit and Lily pressed closer. She could hear her mum's voice squeaking in the background and she wished Dad had put the speaker on.

"Yes, I know, the shelter manager mentioned that. I can't say I'm happy about getting up in the middle of the night but I feel responsible for them. They're so little—"

"Dad, what's the matter?" Lily interrupted. "What's Mum saying? Why can't we do it?"

"Because they're so young they'll need hand-rearing, Lily. Mum isn't sure we'll be up to it – we'd have to get up in the middle of the night, probably."

Lily grabbed his arm. "But I could help! Couldn't I? It's the summer holidays, I don't mind. Dad, please! It's like we were meant to find them – we came along just at the right time. We can't give up on them now!"

Dad sighed. "Did you hear all that?" he said into the phone. "Yes, I know. Maybe she is old enough to help out. You know how much she loves cats!"

"OK." Dad smiled at Lily. "Yes, I'll call the shelter back and tell them." He ended the call and laughed. "Wow. This was definitely not what I was expecting when we came out for a walk this morning."

"We'll put them in here," Amy explained, showing Lily and Dad a cardboard travel box that she'd brought with her. She seemed really nice, Lily thought. She'd told them she remembered Hugo from the shelter

and that he'd grown
into such a handsome,
well-behaved dog.

"I've put a hot-
water bottle in for
them, wrapped up
in some towels. If
they've been without
their mum all day,
they'll be getting really
cold. Kittens this young
can't control their own temperature,
you see. They need their mum's body
heat to keep them warm. Even though
it's been so hot today, if we leave them
here overnight without her, they're at
risk of hypothermia – that's getting too
cold to survive."

"How old do you think they are?"

Lily asked, leaning over to look at the kittens. They were still moving – squirming around and nuzzling at each other – but she was sure they weren't as lively as they had been when they first saw them.

"Hard to say exactly. Maybe two to three weeks? Their eyes are open but they don't look big enough to be walking yet. Soon though."

"They don't look as bright as they did this morning," Dad said.

"I was thinking that, too." Lily bit her lip. "Oh no, maybe we waited for too long for their mum to come back."

Amy shook her head. "I don't think so. I know it sounds hard but the best person to look after them is definitely their mum – she's built for feeding them, cleaning them, keeping them warm. If we take them away from her, we're giving the kittens second-best. Do you see what I mean? So if there'd been any chance that their mum was going to come back and care for them, it was better to let her."

"Dad thinks she might have been run over," Lily said, gazing down at the kittens.

Amy nodded. "It's possible, I'm afraid. Or she may just not have been able to feed them. Either way, I think we have to assume she's not coming back."

She opened the travel box and gently reached in to pick up one of the tabby kittens. Hugo whined and Amy laughed. "You're such a good boy, aren't you? Are you taking over from their mum, Hugo?"

She put the kitten gently into the box and Hugo nosed at the cardboard flaps, clearly making sure that the kitten was all right. "We wouldn't usually put foster kittens with a family who had a dog but this is a bit of an emergency. Now, I'll come back to the house with you, if that's OK, and help you set up a safe pen to keep them in."

Amy picked up the other tabby kitten and Lily watched anxiously as the white kitten gave a feeble mew. The kitten looked so little, left all on his own. "Can I pick this one up?" Lily whispered. He was hardly moving.

"Sure."

Lily picked up the tiny kitten – he wasn't much bigger than her cupped hands – and carefully moved him over to the box. He squirmed around and gave another squeaky breath of a mew but then he cuddled up next to the two tabby kittens again, snuggling against the warmth of the hot-water bottle.

Lily looked up at Dad with shining eyes. "Let's take them home."

Chapter Five

Amy came back to the house to help settle the kittens in. She brought in a big box of equipment from her car – special kitten formula milk and kitten bottles and a litter tray. She explained that the kittens would need feeding about every four hours. "It's a lot of work," she said, looking round at them all. "Are you really sure you can manage?"

Mum was reading the instruction sheets, looking rather anxious. "Oh my goodness, I hadn't even thought about sterilizing," she murmured. "But I suppose it's just like feeding a baby. Have we still got the old sterilizer in the loft?"

Dad grinned. "Yes. Now aren't you grateful that I never sorted all that stuff out to go to the charity shop? I'll go and get it. We need to give them a feed as soon as possible, don't we?"

"Yes, that would be great." Amy looked pleased. "Having a sterilizer will definitely make things easier. Oh!" Amy turned round from the table. Hugo had nudged open the kitchen door and marched in, looking determined.

"Sorry, I'll take him out again."
Mum shook her head. "No, Hugo. You
need to stay away from the kittens. It's
going to be tricky keeping him out,
he's used to having his basket and his
food bowls in here."

"Wait a minute," Dad murmured.
"Look at him. He's not at all bothered
that they're in his kitchen. Even
though we've moved his basket away
from the radiator and put the box
there instead."

Amy nodded. "I think you're right.
And I was going to say that I'd try and
get hold of a special heating pad for
you, to keep the kittens warm but I'm
not sure you're going to need it."

The kittens were still in their
cardboard box, curled up on the hot-

water bottle but now Hugo lay down and curled himself around it, so that they had his warmth, too. The kittens were already pressing up against the side of the box next to him. Even though they were so tiny, their instincts were telling them to warm up.

"Hugo really loves them." Lily smiled. She'd never have expected that Hugo would make a brilliant kitten nurse.

"Right," Amy continued. "I'll show you how to mix the milk powder and feed the kittens. And then – well, for another week or so, until they're old enough to do it themselves, I'm afraid you're going to have to help them wee and poo afterwards."

"That's disgusting!" Carly said, making a horrified face.

Amy laughed. "I know it sounds weird. But mother cats lick their kittens after they've fed them and that tells their bodies to wee or poo, you see. When you're hand-rearing kittens, you have to do everything their mum does. But with cotton wool, dampened with warm boiled water," she added hurriedly.

"Thank goodness for that," Dad murmured.

The white kitten woke up and looked around the dark room. He still couldn't see or smell his mother but at least he was properly warm. He remembered being fed, too, but now he was feeling hungry again. He staggered up on to his paws and mewed, calling for his mother. But instead of a fluffy tabby face, a large white nose came over the side of his box and nuzzled at him.

The kitten sniffed and then sneezed and looked up at the huge creature in confusion. This was most definitely not his mother. Whoever it was felt warm, though, and comforting. The kitten mewed again, asking the big dog for food, and felt his two tabby sisters stirring beside him. They started to call for milk, too.

"Hello, Hugo… Did they wake you up?" a deep voice said, laughing a little.

The kitten moved his head towards the sound and then let out a tiny squeak. Hugo had leaned down again, and picked him up – just the way his mother did – in his jaws. The kitten wriggled as he was lifted from the box but then he found himself between the dog's great paws, cosily nestled against the thick fur of his chest. Forgetting to be hungry for a moment, the kitten snuggled closer and drifted back to sleep.

Upstairs, Lily lay half awake. She'd been dreaming about the kittens and now she couldn't tell whether she was asleep or not. She could hear mewing – pitiful little squeaks – and low voices coming from downstairs. Of course! The night-time feed!

Mum and Dad had worked out that it would be best to feed the kittens at about eleven o'clock before they went to bed, then at three in the morning and then again when they all got up. Dad had said it would only be for a week or so, until the kittens were a bit older and could go for more than four hours without food.

Lily had begged to be allowed to

help but Mum and Dad had said it was far too late for her and Carly, even though it was the holidays.

But if they were feeding the kittens, why could she hear mewing? The little squeaks sounded desperate. Lily sat up worriedly. She had to make sure they were OK – especially the fluffy white one. He had felt so tiny in her hands when she lifted him into the box, as though there was hardly anything of him under all that fur.

Lily got out of bed, pulled on her dressing gown and fumbled sleepily for her slippers. Then she crept down the stairs.

She tiptoed along the hallway and peered into the kitchen. Her mum and dad were sitting at the table in their pyjamas, each with a tabby kitten in their laps. The kittens were busily sucking from the bottles.

"Lily! You should be asleep!" Dad sighed.

"I could hear mewing, it woke me up. What's wrong?"

"It's a bit tricky feeding more than one at once – the white kitten was asleep, so we thought we'd leave him till last but now he's woken up and he's not happy about waiting," Mum explained. "I expect he can smell the milk."

Lily was just about to crouch down and peer into the box when Hugo gave a mournful "Arrrooo!" and she realized that he had the kitten between his paws.

"Oh, Hugo's looking after him!"

"He lifted the kitten out of the box in his mouth," Dad told her. "I was a bit worried. But then I think mother cats do the same thing."

"Is all that mewing bothering you, Hugo?" Lily asked. Then she turned back to look at Mum and Dad. "Shall I feed him? Since I'm awake anyway? We've got another bottle and Hugo's getting upset, you can tell. He doesn't like Stanley crying like that."

"Stanley?" Mum smiled at her. "Since when is he called Stanley?"

Lily went pink. "I just think he looks like a Stanley. It's such a cute name."

"It is cute," Mum agreed, passing Lily a bottle. "But just remember we're not going to have them for long, Lily. Only until the shelter can find a foster home."

"I know." Lily gently scooped up the white kitten and carried him over to the table. Hugo followed her, resting his muzzle on her lap so he could watch what she was doing. Stanley seemed to have learned exactly what to do with the bottle from his two previous feeds – he practically jumped at it, sucking greedily at the milk with funny little slurping noises.

"Wow, you really were hungry," Lily murmured. "Mum, look, I think I can actually see his tummy getting bigger!"

Her mum laughed. "They're really guzzling it down, aren't they. Oh, Lily, listen!"

"I can feel it…" Lily whispered back. Stanley was purring.

Chapter Six

"Which one's your favourite?" Mara leaned over the kitten pen, admiring the three kittens. Lily had emailed her best friend to tell her about their amazing discovery, and Mara had been desperate to come and see the kittens as soon as she'd got back from her holiday in Spain.

They were about five weeks old

now – big enough to walk around really well. They stomped all over each other, squeaking loudly, and they were always wrestling and jumping out at each other. They loved playing with all the toys Lily had persuaded Mum and Dad to get from the pet shop, too. Their favourite was a feathery stick, a bit like a feather duster, and Lily spent ages waving it about for them.

Dad had found a big shallow plastic storage box up in the loft when he was looking for the sterilizer and he'd brought it down to use as a pen to keep the kittens in. It meant they had space to move around but they were safer than they would be loose in the kitchen. But it hadn't lasted long. They still used it to sleep in but they'd learned to wriggle and scramble their way out after just a few days.

"Stanley – he's my favourite," Lily said, pointing him out. "He's like a little fluffy snowball!"

"He is cute," Mara agreed. "But I love the stripes on the other two as well. Isn't it loads of work looking after them all?"

"They're starting to eat proper food now – special kitten food mixed with a bit of their milk. At least that means we can just feed them really late at night and then early in the morning. No one has to get up in the middle of the night any more." Lily reached her hand into the plastic box and Stanley staggered determinedly towards her, licking at her fingers.

"They're so gorgeous. If it was me, I don't think I'd be able to give them away," Mara said, lifting one of the tabby kittens on to her lap. They were both girls, and Carly had named them Bella and Trixie. "You've spent your whole summer holiday looking after them but then you don't get to keep them. That doesn't seem fair!"

"I know." Lily sighed. "But we were never going to keep them. They were originally supposed to go to another foster family as soon as they had the space. But when Amy came to check up on them, a couple of days after they came here, she said we were doing so well maybe we should just keep them until they were ready for rehoming. And luckily Mum and Dad said yes!" She smiled as Stanley butted his head against her hand and let out a squeaky little mew. "It's not food time yet, baby…"

"So they won't go to the shelter, then?"

"Their photos are up on the shelter website already but they'll just send anyone who's interested in adopting them round to us. So at least the kittens won't have to get used to a new place."

Mara nodded. "And I suppose you'll be able to see if the people are nice."

Lily nodded. She didn't like thinking about the kittens' new owners – especially not Stanley's. Even though she was making the best of it to Mara, she couldn't imagine not having a box of kittens in their kitchen… But they already had Hugo.

"Do you think Hugo will miss them?" Mara asked, as she heard scrabbling at the kitchen door.

Lily opened the door, checking that the kittens weren't about to dart through and Hugo trotted in, immediately coming over to inspect his kittens.

"Definitely." Lily stroked his nose. "He does that every time he's been out for a walk. He has to come back and make sure they're all OK. Yes, don't worry, I looked after them for you. Trixie's over there, see?"

Hugo was looking around for the other tabby kitten, and when he spotted her peeking out from behind the kitchen bin he went to round her up, gently nosing her back over towards the plastic box.

"He wants them all in the box the whole time," Lily explained. "He's like a sheepdog, herding them about." She watched proudly as Hugo picked up the tabby kitten in his mouth and dropped her, wriggling, back into the box.

"I thought he was biting her!" Mara said, looking a bit worried.

"No. He's so gentle. He just holds them in his mouth. Their mum would have done the same thing. Oh, Hugo, look, Stanley's coming out now."

The white kitten was clambering out of the box, half falling, half jumping out on to the kitchen tiles. Hugo seemed almost to sigh. He lay down in front of the box between the two girls, making a big furry barrier between Stanley and the rest of the kitchen.

Stanley nuzzled him, nose to nose, and both girls "aaahhed". Stanley marched along the whole length of Hugo and started to pat at his feathery tail as Hugo twitched it from side to side and then jumped on it with fierce little growls. Hugo watched him, clearly enjoying the game. As soon as Stanley was clinging on with all four paws, he swished his tail faster so that the kitten swept across the floor and both girls burst out laughing.

"They go together so well," Mara said. "Both of them white and fluffy."

"I know." Lily nodded. They really did. If only they could keep Stanley, he and Hugo would be a perfect pair.

Lily giggled as Stanley wobbled
down her bed. He wasn't very good at
walking on the squishy duvet and he
kept nearly falling over. He stopped
to inspect her teddy bear and then
jumped at it, sinking his tiny claws into
the ribbon around its neck.

Lily was so busy watching Stanley,
she didn't notice the gentle scuffling
noises from outside her bedroom
window. Then there was a loud hiss
and she glanced round in surprise.
Pixie was standing on the sloping roof,
peering in at the open window, the fur
on the back of her neck raised. She was
clearly furious – this was her place and
now there was another cat.

"Oh, Pixie, no!" Lily stared at her anxiously. What was she going to think of Stanley? She'd been in Lily's room a couple of times since they'd got the kittens but Lily had quickly shut her door so Pixie didn't go downstairs. This was the first time Pixie had seen one of them.

Lily dithered, not sure whether to grab Stanley or try to shoo Pixie out. She didn't want to push her back through the window, in case she slipped. Pixie came further in, climbing on to Lily's windowsill and hissing loudly, her tail fluffing up.

"No!" Lily said sharply, seeing Stanley cower back against the teddy bear, his own fur starting to stand up, too. "Pixie, out! This isn't your house!"

She sat up, trying to grab Pixie.
Perhaps she could take her downstairs
and put her out of the front door. "I
know you've been in here before, I'm
sorry, Pixie. Ow!" Pixie had swiped
her paw down Lily's arm, leaving two
bright red scratches. Then she hissed
again, spat angrily at Stanley and
darted back out of the window.

Lily shut the window, rather shakily.
Pixie had never scratched her before.
Then she glanced round at Stanley.

83

He was huddled into a tiny white ball on her bed and he looked terrified.

"Oh, Stanley, I'm sorry, sweetheart. It's OK. She's not coming back in." Gently, Lily lifted him up in her cupped hands and snuggled him up against her T-shirt.

"It's all right, I'll look after you, shh. I wish I could just look after you always," she added sadly. The shelter had called Mum that morning to say a lady had seen the kittens on their website and wanted to come and visit them. She was interested in the two tabbies but Lily knew it wouldn't be long until someone wanted to take Stanley, too.

Stanley huddled against her, his heart thumping. He didn't understand what had just happened. He had been enjoying playing with Lily by himself, without his sisters climbing all over her, too. He loved it when she fussed over him and played with him and then let him snooze on her lap when he was tired out. But suddenly the other cat had appeared, one that Stanley had never seen before.

Hugo nosed his way round Lily's door and padded across the room.

"Did you hear Pixie?" Lily murmured. "She was really cross. Oh, you can smell her, can't you?"

Hugo's ears had flattened back and he was sniffing at Lily's bed. Then he nudged Stanley gently. The white kitten rubbed his head against the huge dog's muzzle and then stepped back with a squeak as Hugo licked him, his big pink tongue practically covering the tiny kitten.

"Hugo!" Lily giggled. "Look at him, you've flattened his fur!"

"They're so beautiful... I wish we could take all of them but I think three cats might be too many." Candace smiled at Lily and Carly and their mum. "You've done so well, hand-rearing them. They're so big and healthy-looking. You did an amazing job!"

Mum put her arm round Lily's shoulders. "To be honest, it was mostly Lily. She's worked really hard – she even did some of the night feeds. I can't believe how big they are now. Seven weeks old! The time's gone so fast."

Far too fast, Lily thought to herself.

"I suppose if they were still with their mum, it would be too early for us to adopt them," Candace said thoughtfully. "It's very lucky for us, getting to have such small kittens. We're really grateful. Aren't we, Jack?"

Her little boy nodded. He had Bella on his lap and he was running one finger carefully down her back all the way from the top of her head to her tail, over and over. Bella was nuzzling his hand, purring, and Jack looked as though his dream had come true.

Even though Lily hated the thought of someone else taking her lovely kittens home, she could see that Candace and Jack were going to be amazing cat owners. At least they were only taking Bella and Trixie, she thought sadly. She wondered how Stanley would feel all on his own.

Stanley watched, confused, as the strange people put his sisters into a cat

carrier. They were mewing, not sure
what was happening, and he squeaked
back anxiously. Where were they
going? And why wasn't he going, too?

He hurried to the edge of the plastic
box as the kitchen door opened and
they all started to walk out – those
people were taking
his sisters away!
Panicking, he
clawed his way up
the side of the box,
his paws slipping,
and scrambled out
on to the floor to
chase after them. But
the door closed before he
was halfway there, and he sat
under the table and mewed frantically.

He jumped up when the door opened again and Lily let Hugo in. The big dog came nosing under the table and lowered his head to Stanley. He licked the kitten with one great swipe of his huge pink tongue and then slumped down to the floor next to him, resting his muzzle between his paws.

Stanley patted at one of Hugo's long white paws, nibbled it and then snuggled wearily into the kitten-sized space between Hugo's paw and his nose, curling up into a sad little ball.

Chapter Seven

"Night, Mum." Lily peered round her mum's office door on her way to bed. "Oh, that one's so cute. Wow, you can really see how fluffy he's getting." Lily leaned over her mum's shoulder, admiring the photos of Stanley on her computer. "What are you looking at the photos for? Are you sending them to Grandma?" Lily's grandma loved cats, too. She lived in Scotland so she hadn't seen the kittens yet but Lily had been telling her all about them on the phone. Grandma had told Lily how jealous she was.

Her mum looked up. "No, I wasn't. Maybe I should though, I hadn't thought of that. I was actually looking for a good photo to send to Amy for the shelter website. The one they've got up there now is all the kittens together – we need one of just Stanley on his own."

Lily took a step back, suddenly feeling breathless. She knew that Stanley was going to be adopted, too, of course she did. But this made it all too real – and too soon. He looked so cute in the photo on Mum's screen –

he had his mouth open in a mew and
his little pink tongue was showing.
His eyes were shining emerald green
and his fur was standing out around
his head in a fluffy halo. Anybody
would want to adopt him, Lily thought
miserably. Who could resist such a
gorgeous boy?

"Oh, Lily…" Mum turned round
in her chair, reaching out to hug her.
"I know you love him…"

"Couldn't we keep him?" Lily pleaded. "He's so special…" Her voice wobbled and her throat felt like it was closing up. She couldn't get any more words out.

"You know we were only looking after them for a little while, darling."

Lily nodded and sniffed and then dashed out of Mum's office, racing upstairs to her bedroom. She flung herself down on her bed, burying her face in her pillow, her eyes full of tears. Why couldn't they keep Stanley? He got on amazingly with Hugo. Mara had been right when she said they made a perfect pair. Hugo had looked after Stanley all morning after Bella and Trixie had gone. In fact, Lily was pretty sure that Hugo would be as upset as her if Stanley went to a new home.

She just had to explain all that properly to Mum and Dad. Lily rubbed her eyes and sniffed determinedly. Maybe she should write down a list of reasons to keep Stanley, just to make sure she didn't forget any of them. And then she would find just the right time to convince her family…

Lily woke up suddenly, her heart racing. She sat up in bed and peered around anxiously, trying to work out what was wrong. Everything in her room looked strange and ghostly in the darkness. Why had she jumped awake like that?

She was just about to settle down again, fussing with the crumpled sheet and wishing the night wasn't so hot, when loud barking erupted downstairs – mixed with ear-splitting yowls. Hugo was obviously furious, it was his angry bark, over and over again – and then there was a crashing sound.

Lily flung back the sheet and headed downstairs at a run, not even stopping to think what was going on. Something awful was happening. She could hear voices in Mum and Dad's room – they'd clearly been woken up, too, and Carly appeared in her bedroom doorway as Lily started down the stairs.

She was surprised to see the kitchen door was open but then realized that

Mum and Dad must have left it ajar to keep the room a bit cooler for Hugo and Stanley to sleep in. Hugo wouldn't come out of the kitchen anyway, he loved his basket. But maybe Stanley had come out of the kitchen and got lost in the dark. Had that crash been him knocking something over in the living room, maybe? That wouldn't make Hugo react so badly though, would it? He was still barking – quieter barks now and furious growls. Lily couldn't remember ever hearing him so upset.

Lily switched on the kitchen light, murmuring, "Stanley? Hugo? What's the matter?" Then she gasped. The kitchen looked as though someone had run round pushing everything that they could find off the surfaces. The pile of newspapers from the recycling box was scattered all over the place. The vase of flowers that had been in the middle of the kitchen table was tipped over, cascading water down on to the tiles. There was even a mug smashed on the floor just below the sink.

Hugo was standing in front of the sink, growling angrily at the window above it. Lily shivered, suddenly wondering if there had been someone in the garden? Perhaps Hugo had been woken by a burglar? Could he have made all this mess just by jumping about, trying to raise the alarm? Even though he wasn't usually clumsy, he did sometimes knock things over by flailing his tail around when he was really excited.

"It's OK, Hugo, shh," Lily murmured. "What's wrong? And where's Stanley?" she added. When she'd gone to bed, Stanley had been curled up in Hugo's basket, snuggled in between Hugo's paws, and both of them had been asleep. There was no little white kitten in the dog basket now, or in the big plastic box.

"Stanley?" Lily called worriedly. Where was he? She ducked down, searching under the table and behind the bin but there was no little white kitten.

"Lily, what's going on?" Dad hurried into the kitchen, with Mum and Carly close behind. "Wow! What happened here?"

"I don't know! Hugo's really upset and I can't find Stanley. He isn't anywhere."

Hugo came over to Dad, sniffing and nosing at his hands, and Dad rubbed his ears comfortingly. "Hey, he's got a scratch on his nose," Dad said. "What happened, boy?"

"Oh, Hugo, did you cut yourself on that broken mug?" Mum crouched down to look, too.

Hugo pulled away and padded over to the sink cabinet again, this time leaping up and planting his paws on the edge of the sink. He wasn't supposed to jump up like that but nobody stopped him.

Then a little white face peered out from behind the curtains. Stanley – with his long white fur all fluffed up. He was huddling in the corner of the windowsill, looking terrified.

"There he is!" Lily exclaimed gratefully. "How on earth did you get up there?" She hurried over to the windowsill, picking up Stanley and cuddling him close. She'd never have thought that Stanley could make the jump on to the counter – he must have jumped on to a chair to get him halfway. "Come on, Stanley, it's OK. What happened?"

"It's pretty obvious," Dad said anxiously. "They've been fighting. Hugo couldn't have cut his nose on that mug, not unless it actually fell on him. That's a cat scratch."

Lily could feel the white kitten's heart hammering and his ears were laid back. Hugo dropped back down to the floor and stood looking up at

Stanley in Lily's arms.

"That can't be right," Lily said, shaking her head. "Stanley loves Hugo. They were even asleep together in Hugo's basket when I went to bed! And Hugo wouldn't hurt Stanley."

"He didn't!" Carly said angrily, crouching down beside Hugo and putting her arm round him. "Stanley hurt *him*! Look at his poor nose!"

Mum sighed. "We don't know which of them started it. I suppose we've been lucky we haven't had any issues with them until now – it's weird this has happened so suddenly... But if they're going to start fighting with each other, we'll have to talk to Amy in the morning. Stanley's old enough to stay at the shelter now until they find a home for him. Hopefully they've got room."

"What?" Lily gasped. "No, Mum, he's staying here. We said we'd look after him until we found him a proper home. He can't go to the shelter!"

"He has to, Lily," Dad said gently. "I know you've loved having the kittens here and you've worked so hard with them but we can't risk Stanley being hurt if he and Hugo aren't getting on. What if Stanley tries to scratch Hugo again and Hugo lashes out? I know Hugo wouldn't deliberately hurt him – at least, I don't think he would – but he's just so much bigger than Stanley. It's not safe."

"And this is Hugo's home!" Carly put in.

"She's right, Lily," Dad said. "We can't send Hugo away."

Lily shook her head, tears starting to well up in her eyes. Stanley wriggled a little as one fell on to his nose and he licked it, liking the salty taste.

This couldn't be happening, Lily thought, looking miserably from Dad to Mum to Carly. Everyone seemed to be certain that Stanley had to go. How could this be happening now? Tomorrow was supposed to be the start of her grand plan to convince everyone they could keep their gorgeous kitten forever – and now instead he was going to be sent to the shelter.

"He just can't," she whispered. "He'll hate it there. We saw the cats when we went to get Hugo – they had those little rooms. He's used to a whole big kitchen and my bedroom. He'll be so lonely without us." *And without Hugo*, Lily added in her head. She still couldn't understand what had happened. Hugo had never barked at the kittens – not even when he'd first found them in the woods. He'd looked after them so carefully – Stanley even slept in his basket. This just wasn't right.

But nobody was listening to her. It felt like all the plans were already made – Mum and Dad were discussing who could go and drop off Stanley at the shelter. Carly was still petting Hugo and glaring at the kitten.

"What are we going to do with them tonight?" Dad murmured, looking between Stanley and Hugo. "We can't leave them both in here, obviously."

"I'll take Stanley upstairs with me," Lily said quickly. It was their last night, she realized. Her last time to cuddle him. "I'll take his box upstairs with me and put it by my bed."

Mum nodded. "OK. But shut your door, Lily."

"I'll bring the box for you," Dad said. He picked it up and followed her up the stairs.

Lily couldn't help crying into Stanley's fur as she took him up to her room. He was still so little – far too little to go to the shelter, she was sure. It would be like sending him off for his first day of school. She half laughed, half sniffed at the thought.

"I'm really going to miss this one," Dad said, rubbing one finger under Stanley's chin as Lily climbed into bed, still holding him. She put him down gently on top of the sheet and Stanley started to wander around the folds, his paws sliding.

"Oh, Lily, don't cry, sweetheart." Dad put his arm round her. "He'll go to a lovely new home. He's so gorgeous, he probably won't even be in the shelter for a day."

"I don't want him to have a lovely new home," Lily sobbed. "I want him to stay here!"

"I know." Dad sighed. "I had been thinking that, too… But this is Hugo's home, Lily, love. You know that."

"I still can't believe they were fighting…" Lily whispered.

Stanley came stomping back up the bed towards her and began to clamber on to her legs, wriggling as he got caught up in the sheet. Dad laughed and helped him up with a hand under his bottom. "There you go, Stanley. Night, Lily." He went over to close the bedroom window. "Just in case – we don't want Stanley getting out. I hope it's not too hot. Everything will be OK, honestly."

Lily watched him go, blowing her a kiss from the doorway and then closing the door behind him. *How can everything possibly be OK?* she thought sleepily, as Stanley padded round and round on her tummy, making himself a comfy little nest. *It's not OK at all…*

Stanley tucked his nose under his tail and closed his eyes. He loved the feeling of snuggling up on top of Lily. He could tell that there was something wrong, her breathing sounded different, with strange little hitches that made him bounce on her tummy each time. But he'd never been able to sleep on her bed before – it was even better than curling up next to Hugo. He was warm and safe…

His ears flattened back for a moment

as he suddenly remembered and he let out a little mew of fright. He'd been fast asleep and then the barking had woken him. Stanley had never heard Hugo bark like that before – he was protecting his house. He'd been trying to protect Stanley, too, but the noise was still so scary.

Stanley had run madly around the kitchen, trying to find a hiding place but nowhere had felt safe. In the end he'd jumped on to the kitchen table and then made a flying leap on to the counter, scrabbling madly and nearly falling back down. He'd huddled himself behind the curtains, curling up as small as he could as the barking and hissing went on and on.

Stanley stood up, pacing round and

round on the bed to calm himself down. Lily shifted a little, with a wheezy moan, and settled again. Then, at last, they slept.

Chapter Eight

"Do you think they'll want his toys at the shelter?" Mum said doubtfully, holding up a catnip mouse with half its tail gone and a hole where the stuffing was coming out.

"He loves that mouse," Lily said, with a catch in her voice. "You have to take it!" She abandoned her cereal – she wasn't hungry anyway – and got down on the kitchen floor, looking for all the jingly balls, feathers and other toys that were scattered about. Of course, Stanley's favourite toy was Hugo, she realized, looking at them both under the table. Mum and Dad had decided that as long as someone stayed with them both the whole time, it was OK to let them be in the same room until Mum took Stanley to the shelter.

Hugo was lying full length under the table – probably hoping for Carly's toast crusts – and Stanley was playing with his paws. He was hopping over them, pouncing and patting at them with his own. Every so often Hugo would yawn and move a paw a little, so that Stanley leaped on it with ferocious tigerish growls.

Mum kept turning round from the bacon she was cooking and glancing over at them, obviously checking that they weren't about to fight again but they weren't. It was a game, it always was. Lily stared at them, trying not to let herself start crying again. She still couldn't quite believe that this was happening. How could they be happy together now, when Hugo had been so furious last night and Stanley so terrified?

"Can you get that, Lily?" Mum said, as the doorbell rang. "I don't want to leave this pan. It's probably just the post."

Lily got up and went to the door, opening it just as her dad came downstairs. Their next-door neighbour, Anna, was standing there, looking worried.

"Hi, Anna." Dad came over to the door. "Is everything all right?"

Anna smiled. "I hope so… But I've come to apologize, just in case."

"OK…" Dad said, looking puzzled. "Would you like some coffee? We're just having breakfast."

"Oh, I didn't mean to interrupt!"

"Honestly, it's fine."

"I'd love a coffee." Anna smiled, and followed Lily and Dad through to the kitchen, where Mum was dishing out the bacon.

"I do feel bad, though," Anna continued. "I've a horrible feeling that Pixie's been in here again. She bolted in through the cat flap at about midnight, in a bit of a state. She was soaking wet and all the fur that wasn't plastered down with water was sticking up. And I heard a lot of barking, so I wondered if she'd climbed through Lily's window again and had had a bit of a bust-up with Hugo… You mentioned she'd come in that way before."

Anna looked between Mum and Dad as the whole family stared at her. "I really am sorry," she added. "I know she's a nightmare. My neighbours on the other side got quite cross with her the other day – they found her on the kitchen table licking the butter…" Her voice trailed away. "Oh no, what did she do?"

"It was Pixie!" Lily breathed, remembering her open bedroom window. "It was Pixie, not Stanley! Hugo was barking at Pixie!" And that meant Stanley didn't need to go…

"Mum, do you think…?" Lily put her hand on Mum's arm, trying to get her to listen, but Mum was looking at Anna and not paying attention.

"She was in here, then. Oh dear…"
Anna looked around the kitchen. "I
really hope she didn't break anything."

Dad laughed. "Actually, I think she
broke a mug but don't worry, Anna.
That's about the best news you could
have given us. We came down last
night because Hugo was barking his
head off to find the kitchen in a bit
of a mess and Hugo with a scratch on
his nose. No, no, it's OK!" he added,
seeing Anna put a hand up to her
mouth. "You see, we thought it was
Stanley who'd done it. We were going
to take him to the animal shelter this
morning and now we don't have to!"

"Pixie scratched Hugo?" Anna
looked down at Hugo guiltily. "Poor
Hugo. She's a horror, she really is."

"But you love her to bits," Mum said, laughing.

"I'd better start locking the cat flap at night." Anna sighed.

"Mum." Lily pulled at her sleeve. "Mum, listen, please, it's important. You need to call the shelter."

Mum gave her a hug. "It's OK, Lily, you don't need to tell me. We'll call them right now and let them know we don't need to bring Stanley in after all."

"I should have listened when you said that Hugo wouldn't have been barking like that at Stanley," Dad said, shaking his head. "I mean just look at them."

Everyone looked down under the table. Stanley, worn out from his game, was collapsed over Hugo's enormous paws. As they stared at him, he opened one eye lazily, just a slit of green peering up at them all.

"Please…" Lily whispered. "Couldn't we keep him? I know we had Hugo first but Hugo loves him, too."

"Can we?" Carly put in. "It would make Hugo sad if he had to go," she admitted. "I think Stanley should stay."

"Yes! Oh, Carly, thank you!" Lily hugged her sister tight.

Mum smiled. "I'd better go and ring the shelter, hadn't I?"

"What are you going to say to them?" Lily asked anxiously.

"I'm going to ask them to take his photo off the website – he's already got a home."

Lily threw her arms
round her mum and
then her dad and
even Anna –
she wanted to
hug everyone.
Then she
crouched down
beside Stanley
and Hugo. "You're
staying," she said,
stroking the fluffy white
fur on Stanley's tummy.
You're our kitten now!"

Stanley opened the other eye and
stretched, rolling over on to his back
and padding his front paws against
Hugo's nose. Hugo snorted, shifted his
head and gently licked the little kitten.

Stanley uncurled himself from the big dog and stood up, stretching again and arching his back as he yawned. He padded deliberately over to Lily, and rubbed the side of his head lovingly up and down her shorts. He climbed on to her knees and stood up, nudging her chin with the top of his head and purring loudly. Then he jumped down and touched noses with Hugo.

"They're perfect," Lily whispered, crouching down to stroke Hugo. "They belong together, here with us."

Out Now:

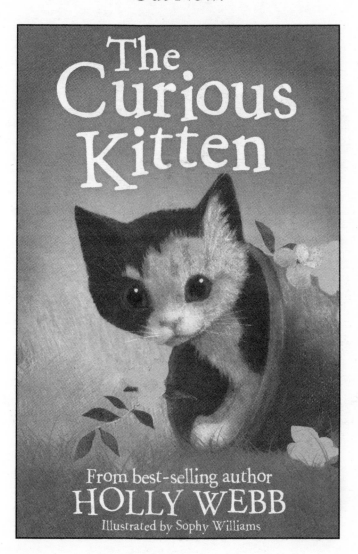

The
Curious
Kitten

From best-selling author
HOLLY WEBB
Illustrated by Sophy Williams

HOLLY WEBB

Holly Webb started out as a children's book editor and wrote her first series for the publisher she worked for. She has been writing ever since, with over one hundred books to her name. Holly lives in Berkshire, with her husband and three young sons. Holly's pet cats are always nosying around when she is trying to type on her laptop.

For more information
about Holly Webb visit:

www.holly-webb.com